If I hadn't been so intent on showing off everything I knew about Central Park, I might have been able to prevent what happened next. As the riders got closer to us, one of their horses must have spotted Zoey. The horse screamed in fright and reared.

The awful sound startled me. Zoey grabbed my leg with one hand. Her other hand clutched mine tightly. I saw the rider try to keep her horse under control, but it was no use. The horse screamed again.

The sound was so terrifying that I threw my hands over my ears and shut my eyes. After a while I felt hands trying to pull mine away from my head.

"Molly! Open your eyes!" It was Tyler.

I opened them. Tyler was pale. I saw Brad standing next to him. Brad was green.

About a yard away, the rider of the nervous horse was standing next to him, patting his neck. Her rider friends stood with their horses. All of them were looking at us.

There was only one person missing.

"Where's Zoey?" I asked, my heart sinking even as I asked.

"She's gone," Tyler said.

Zoey & Me

Stop That Orangutan!

Zoey & Me

Stop That Orangutan!

MALLORY TARCHER

Troll

Zoey & Me

Stop That Orangutan!

Chapter 1

"**H**aunted! The museum is haunted? No way!"

The mound of mashed potatoes hanging from the end of my fork plopped onto my plate. I felt a drop of gravy hit the end of my nose. Without thinking, I wiped it off with my sleeve.

Grandpa pushed his own plate away from him and folded his hands on the table. I didn't like the frown on his face one little bit, or the way he was hanging his head. For the very first time I could remember, Grandpa looked . . . *old*.

"Well, Molly," he said, "that's what some people are saying."

I stuck my empty fork in my mouth and almost stabbed myself. I forgot I'd lost my mashed potatoes. I put the fork down. Who could eat at a time like this?

My mother reached out and put her hand on her father's arm. She was sitting next to Grandpa at the big round dining-room table that he and Grandma bought when they were first married, about a bazillion years ago.

"Dad, why don't you start at the beginning," she said calmly.

"Yeah, Grandpa, maybe we can help."

My eyes widened as I looked at my brother, Brad. Help? Since when did Brad care about anyone besides himself? Okay, I was being unfair, but I was still getting used to the idea that my once totally and completely obnoxious brother was becoming kind of like a human being. I mean, he had really come through for me and for Zoey only a few weeks before when Zoey had to go to the Northern Ohio Zoo . . .

I'll get to *that* story in a minute.

"Yes, Professor Hood," Tyler Matthews, my best friend in the world, agreed. Then, nodding toward Brad and me, he added, "We're not professional detectives, but the three of us are pretty good at solving crimes."

I beamed at Tyler. We've known each other forever. He lives next door to me back home in Los Angeles, and we're in the same class at school. Up until about a year ago, I thought of Tyler like a brother—a *normal* brother. But then, something changed. It's kind of embarrassing to admit, but almost every time I look at him I start feeling sort of goopy. Sometimes I stare at his ear, and I can't stop. Weird. Luckily, Tyler doesn't seem to notice, and I don't ever want him to! It could be the end of our friendship, and the *last* thing I want is to lose Tyler as my best friend.

Just then, Grandpa's live-in housekeeper, Mrs. Nelson, came into the dining room. Everybody sat up straight, even Grandpa. I've known Mrs. Nelson for about as long as I've known Grandpa, but I'm still a little scared of her. Everybody is. Even though she's almost as old as Grandpa, she treats him like he's her child. She tells him to wear a coat when it's cold and to carry an umbrella when it's raining, and she makes sure he eats three meals a day. Some adults probably would hate being bossed around that way, but Grandpa doesn't seem to mind. Now that Grandma is gone, he needs someone to remind him to comb his hair and make sure his socks match.

See, Grandpa's sort of a flaky professor. He's so superintelligent, he's always thinking about philosophy and science and other complicated subjects. He can't be bothered with remembering lots of small details, things like taking his keys or wallet with him when he goes out.

I guess it makes sense that he's been the director of the museum of natural history in New York for years. Grandpa's work means everything to him, and for some reason, his absentmindedness disappears at the office—which is why his announcement about the museum's being haunted was so weird.

"Well," Mrs. Nelson said in her deep voice, "there'd better be a good explanation for your not having finished your dinner, young lady."

"Uhh . . ." I began.

But Mrs. Nelson, hands on her hips and a frown on her broad face, wasn't talking to me. She was staring down at Zoey.

"Zoey's probably just tired from the long trip, Mrs. Nelson," my mom said quickly. Nobody wanted to insult Mrs. Nelson's cooking.

11

"Yeah," I added. "Usually, she'll eat *anything*." I blushed. "Uh, what I mean is . . ."

I didn't finish my sentence, which is probably a good thing. If you haven't already guessed, my brain is medium-sized, but my mouth is extra-large. It gets me into a lot of trouble.

Zoey saved the day. With a low grunt, she took her fork and scooped up the rest of the food on her plate. In one huge gulp, she finished. Then she put her fork down and looked up at Mrs. Nelson with a little grin. I could have sworn she was waiting for a pat on the head.

Mrs. Nelson dropped her hands from her hips and smiled.

"Now, that's more like it," she said as she began to gather empty dinner plates in a stack.

I couldn't believe it! Zoey, my one-year-old baby orangutan sister, who's afraid of no one and nothing, was as afraid of Mrs. Nelson as I was!

Grandpa hadn't said anything since Mom had asked him to tell us the whole story about what was going on at the museum. After Mrs. Nelson had cleared the table and served dessert, Mom touched Grandpa's arm again.

"Dad?"

Grandpa took a sip of his coffee.

"Um," he said. "Strong and black. Just the way I like it." He winked at me. "Puts hair on your back!"

This was one of our old routines.

"Ewww!" I wailed.

Grandpa laughed. Suddenly, he didn't seem so old anymore.

"Dad, the hauntings?" Mom prompted.

"Yes, of course." Grandpa cleared his throat and went on. "Well, about a month ago, strange things started happening at the museum, sometimes during the day and sometimes at night, after visiting hours. For example, one of the guards, a fine employee who's been with the museum for about ten years, reported seeing one of the figures in an exhibit about prehistoric people move. According to Jake, the figure looked at him and raised a rock, as if it were going to throw it through the glass. . . ."

Grandpa shook his head. "I tried to convince Jake he was imagining things, that maybe he needed a vacation, but he swore he'd seen what he'd seen. Then other guards also reported hearing odd noises—like animals howling and people chanting. I ordered an investigation, of course. My assistant director, Mr. Eelio, was in charge, and he found nothing. He believed that the guards just wanted to cause trouble because they were angry about their new work schedules. After he spoke to all of them about the matter, two of the guards quit—and one was Jake. Now I can't help but wonder if I did the right thing."

"Go on, Grandpa," I said. "Tell us what happened then."

I scooted my chair closer to Zoey's so that she could climb onto my lap. I'd seen her eyes closing and knew I should put her to bed, but I didn't want to miss a word of Grandpa's story.

Grandpa continued, his voice grim. "Things only

got worse. One of our newest mineral exhibits was vandalized, and several precious dinosaur artifacts on display were damaged. . . . I don't know how any of the incidents happened or who is responsible."

"Have you called in the police?" Mom asked.

Grandpa shook his head. "No. Mr. Eelio has advised me against calling too much attention to the incidents. The last thing the museum needs—the last thing *I* need—is a swarm of police in the museum," he said. "The publicity would be damaging, and daily attendance would suffer. We have school groups visiting every day, and so many special programs and activities—"

"But what *are* you doing, Professor Hood?" Tyler asked as he leaned forward across the dinner table. I recognized that look of determination. I stared at the lock of blond hair that hung over Tyler's left eye. I watched in fascination as he brushed it off his face.

I shut my mouth with a snap. My jaw had been hanging open about a mile. What was wrong with me?

Grandpa rubbed the back of his neck and sighed. "Well, that's just it, Tyler. I have to meet with the museum board this Friday and report on our findings, but frankly, I don't have anything to tell them. I was hoping that the incidents would stop, but . . ."

"But what?" Tyler prodded.

"Last night, something else happened," Grandpa said. "One of the guards thought he heard a suspicious noise coming from one of the workrooms. He tried to investigate, but before he could use his key to get into the room . . . someone came up behind him and hit him on the head. Another guard found him a few hours later and got him to the hospital. Luckily, he wasn't badly hurt, but the workroom was torn apart."

"Was anything missing?" Brad asked.

"Unfortunately," Grandpa explained, "the room is always such a mess, we still can't tell. It could be that a few of the fossils we can't find are somewhere in the room. We should know by tomorrow."

"This has gotten far too dangerous not to call in the police, Dad," my mom said. I could tell by her face that she was really worried.

I had to agree with her. I felt really bad for the guard who'd gotten hit on the head, but what if it had been my grandfather? I shuddered and held Zoey closer.

Obviously, Grandpa didn't agree. He was shaking his head so hard, his wispy gray hair looked like antennae flying around his head.

"No, I can't do that. Not yet. Mr. Eelio is right. The negative publicity that would come along with a police investigation would seriously hurt the museum's business, and . . . well, it wouldn't look too good for me right now either," Grandpa admitted. "In all my years as director, I've never had this kind of trouble. Never. I have to try every way I know how to get to the bottom of these events before I call in the police."

"Dad—"

Grandpa held up his hand. "I promise that if I can't find the culprit by the end of the week, I'll suggest to the board that they order a full police investigation."

"It's already Monday night, Grandpa," Brad pointed out. "That doesn't leave you much time."

"Do you suspect it's an inside job?" Tyler asked.

Grandpa shrugged. "Who would want to sabotage the museum? And why? Every member of my staff is one hundred percent loyal. No, I think whoever is responsible is not connected with the museum in any way."

"There's another possibility," I piped in. "Maybe the museum *is* haunted. Maybe a ghost is responsible—"

The glares I was getting from Mom, Brad, Tyler, and my dad (who'd been very quite through all of this) shut me up. Fast.

Grandpa laughed. "No, Molly, I'm pretty sure we're dealing with a flesh-and-blood criminal."

I had to regain my dignity. I stood up, a sleeping, drooling, two-foot-long orangutan hanging awkwardly from my arms.

"We'll find the bad guys, Grandpa," I vowed. "It's a promise."

Just then, Zoey burped. Loudly.

"See," I said brightly. "Even Zoey promises!"

Chapter

2

I guess it's not fair to start telling a story in the middle, so let me give you some background. My name is Molly Miles. I'm twelve years old and live in Los Angeles, California, with my mom, dad, and brother, Brad. And Zoey.

You've already met Brad. There's not a lot to say about him except that he's a sports nut, and until recently, all we did was fight. I mean, constantly. Lately, though, we can have an entire conversation—with Brad, that always includes lots of "huhs" and "whatevers" and "dunnos"—without tearing each other's head off. Pretty cool.

My mom is the best mother there is. She's a primatologist at the Los Angeles Zoo. That means she studies and works with certain kinds of apes. She loves her job and does it really well. She also takes great care of us, though I pretty much take care of myself.

My dad is a pediatrician. Everybody thinks he's terrific, including me. He's funny and smart and hardly ever gets angry, even when one of us does something stupid. Even *I* occasionally do something stupid—about three or four times a week.

Okay, so you're wondering why such an ordinary family like us comes with an orangutan. It happened like this. A little more than a year ago, one of the orangutans at the Los Angeles Zoo, a female named Lucky, gave birth. That baby orangutan was Zoey.

Because Lucky had grown up in captivity, she didn't understand how to be a mother. My mom explained to us how that happens sometimes with animals who grow up outside their natural habitat. They don't have the opportunity to learn basic behaviors they would have learned in the wild. If Lucky had grown up in the rain forest of Sumatra, my mom told us, she would have watched orangutan mothers with their babies and figured out what to do when she became a mother. But Lucky didn't grow up in Sumatra. She grew up in a zoo. So when Zoey was born, Lucky was very confused and didn't know how to be a mother.

Before we knew it, we found ourselves raising Zoey, and she became the youngest member of the Miles family.

The weirdest thing about our new family member was not that Zoey was an orangutan but that she was a *baby*. I hate to admit it, but for a while, I was pretty jealous of all the attention Zoey was getting. Before Zoey came to live with us, *I'd* been the baby of the family—and the only girl. Suddenly, I was a big sister, and someone else was playing with my old dolls. I found myself comparing my baby pictures with Zoey's. We both had red hair—all the women in my family do!— and for a while, I was convinced that Zoey's straight, orangy-red fur was much prettier than my own curly, reddish-red hair.

But before long I fell in love with Zoey and couldn't imagine life without her. And life without her almost happened. Just before going to visit Grandpa in New York City, we came close to losing Zoey.

I had just celebrated my twelfth birthday, and Zoey was getting ready to celebrate her first, when we got word that she was being transferred to a dinky little zoo in Ohio. My mother explained to us that even before Zoey was born, she'd been promised to the other zoo as part of an exchange set up by the Species Survival Plan—a program that helps ensure that endangered species survive and thrive. It has a lot to do with breeding, and Zoey had been promised to this other zoo for breeding purposes. We were stuck. Nobody, not even my mom, could figure a way out of the deal. So Zoey went. The worst part was that the people who ran the zoo were *really* mean to the animals.

It took some major scheming, but Tyler, Brad, and I—and a fabulous girl named Sloane Barnes whom I met through the Internet—got the bad guys thrown out of the Northern Ohio Zoo. A few days later, Zoey was home safe with us. One of her cousins, a four-year-old male named Charlie, was going to be transferred from Ohio to the Los Angeles Zoo the following month.

The whole thing taught me that when you really care about something—or someone—you should never give up. We gathered kids from practically all over the country to protest the bad conditions at the Northern Ohio Zoo. We really made a difference. That's why when Grandpa told us about the mystery at the museum, I promised we'd solve it for him. We'd made a difference once. Why couldn't we do it again?

When we got back from Ohio, Mom and Dad started to get us organized for our trip to New York City. Grandpa had invited the family to his retirement party and to stay with him in his huge apartment on Riverside Drive in Manhattan. The apartment had ten rooms and was filled with all sorts of things Grandpa had brought back from his travels around the world— African masks, Indian wall hangings, South American pottery, even an old wooden bench from a medieval church in France!

There was enough cool stuff in Grandpa's apartment to keep anyone busy for days. But I knew we'd also spend some time seeing the sights. Brad and I had been to New York City lots of times, but this trip was going to be special. Zoey was coming with us!

While Zoey was stuck in Ohio with me and Mom, the orangutans at the Los Angeles Zoo had caught an influenza bug. In other words, they all had bad colds, and Zoey wasn't allowed to stay with them until they were better.

Then came the best part. Tyler's parents had decided to take a second honeymoon, so Tyler was coming, too!

"Tyler, are you okay?" I peered into my best friend's

face. What I saw was not good. Tyler was a very unflattering shade of green.

"Uh."

"Oh." I sat back in my window seat and dug into the snack the flight attendant had just served us. Squishy stuff with gray stuff.

Tyler didn't tell me until the morning of our trip that he had never been to New York City. And it wasn't until we were standing in the airport that he admitted he'd never flown.

I didn't tease him about it, though. I just made sure to point out—about a hundred times—where his life jacket was stored. I know it was mean, but I think he looks adorable when he's nervous.

"You know," I said to Tyler, as I chewed vigorously on the gray stuff, "this isn't half bad. It only looks gross. Here, maybe you should try to eat something."

Mistake. With a look of total desperation, Tyler lurched from his seat and tore up the narrow aisle toward the bathroom.

From her seat across the aisle, my mother gave me The Look.

"What!" I protested. "What did I do?"

"You enjoy torturing him, don't you?" Brad said, eyeing me carefully over the top of the seat in front of me. "There's something warped about you, Mol."

"Look who's talking!" I cried, finally swallowing the gray stuff. It wasn't so tasty, after all.

"Okay, children, that's enough," my dad said. Whenever he called Brad and me "children," we shut up. It was no mystery why Dad was annoyed. Zoey had finally fallen asleep, in the seat next to Brad's, but before she had, well . . .

Because of Zoey, we had to travel in First Class. In fact, the zoo had to buy *all* the seats in First Class. Our last experience of traveling with Zoey made it clear to us that people don't like sitting next to an orangutan. Now, knowing that, Dad should have been clued in on how tough the trip might be. But nothing could have prepared him for Zoey's slipping past us, entering the coach section, opening a bathroom door marked "Occupied"—how did she do it?—reaching inside, and tearing the toupee off a man's head.

Wait. It gets worse. The man came bursting out of the bathroom, still pulling up his pants and fumbling with his belt. He was calling Zoey terrible names.

While this was happening, we stood frozen by our seats, mouths open. Tyler, of course, sat in his seat, his mouth open for a very different reason.

As we watched in horror, Zoey leaped onto the lap of a seated passenger and plopped the toupee on that man's very bald head. It was awful. The man bellowed. The first man continued to scream. People were laughing, and two obnoxious ten-year-olds were trying to grab Zoey.

"Look at the shaggy monkey!" one of them shouted.

That did it. No one calls Zoey a monkey. I marched down the aisle, ignoring the angry glares of the flight attendants in coach.

Calmly, I lifted Zoey off the second man's lap and

into my arms. I turned to the obnoxious ten-year-old.

"For your information," I said to his pudgy, sticky face, "Zoey is an orangutan, not a monkey. An orangutan is an endangered species. Please do not touch her."

Then I turned back to the two bald men and—in my very best "I am so sorry, I'm only a little girl, please don't be mad at me" voice—I apologized.

The second man mumbled something I took to be an acceptance of my apology. I nodded graciously. I'm pretty sure the first man would have preferred to throttle me, but he, too, mumbled, "Okay."

"Everything's fine now," I said brightly, settling a suddenly sleepy Zoey into her seat and strapping her in. Tightly.

Dad put his hand to his head and sank into his seat. Brad snickered, Mom sighed, and Tyler groaned.

Having a baby sister who just happens to be an orangutan has its advantages. There was no way a New York City cab driver was going to take an orangutan into Manhattan—without charging five hundred dollars!—so Grandpa had arranged for a limousine from a private car service to pick us up at JFK Airport.

Talk about traveling in style! There was something for everyone. Brad was obsessed with the little color TV. He sat in the seat right behind the driver, facing the back of the car and changing channels about a million times, just like he does at home.

Tyler seemed fully recovered. He sat in the backseat

and plastered his face against one of the side windows. Every two minutes he found something fascinating to point out. "Look at that!" he'd shout, but by the time I looked, we'd already passed whatever bridge or building or billboard had caught his attention. Two minutes later, I'd hear, "Look at that!" again. After a while, I stopped trying to see what he was so excited about. After all, *I* had been to New York City lots of times.

Finally, after about an hour, we pulled up in front of Grandpa's building on Riverside Drive at 107th Street. For a moment, I thought Tyler would pass out. So far, this trip had almost killed him.

"Wow!" he said, standing on the sidewalk with his head thrown back. "It's so tall!"

"Duh." I rolled my eyes. "Of course it's tall. Wait until you see the Empire State Building and the World Trade Center," I said, tossing my hair. Some people are *so* unsophisticated.

There we stood on the sidewalk, the six of us and about six tons of luggage. I don't know who brought more clothes, Tyler or me. The doorman, who was the same guy Brad and I used to terrorize when we were little kids, turned pale when he saw us.

I waved. "Hi, Fred!" I shouted. "We're back!"

"And he looks so thrilled," Tyler mumbled. "Do you have to shout in public, Mol? It's kind of embarrassing."

I stared at my best friend. "Hello? And you're Mr. Sophisticated?" I said. "Mr. I-have-to-barf-the-minute-I-get-on-the-plane?"

"Molly, that's not very nice," Mom scolded.

I frowned. She was right. Mothers always are.

"Okay, I'm sorry, Tyler," I said as I hefted one of my bags into my arms. "Truce?"

"Truce." Tyler picked up two bags and followed me into the lobby. I'd always loved the lobby. It was old but still fancy, and somehow it made me feel as if I were important.

When all six of us had piled into the elevator—Fred had agreed to take our luggage up to the eleventh floor in the freight elevator—I smirked at Tyler.

"Don't say it," he warned.

"What, me?" I raised my eyebrows. "I'm shocked you'd think I'd mention your delicate stomach as we soar eleven stories off the ground . . ."

"Molly!" This time, it was Mom *and* Dad.

At least Zoey appreciates me, I thought, patting her on the head.

When we reached the sixth floor, the elevator stopped to let on a passenger. The door opened to reveal Mrs. Leadbetter and her yappy little dog, Mr. Marc. I couldn't believe someone hadn't strangled that dog yet.

Mrs. Leadbelly—I mean, Leadbetter—stepped onto the elevator and nodded coldly at my parents. What had we ever done to her?

And then she saw Zoey.

"Oh, my!" she cried, clutching her chest.

"Yap, yap, yap, yap . . ." Mr. Marc pulled back his lips and snarled.

I held my breath. What would Zoey do? As far as I knew, Zoey had never met a mean animal.

Zoey picked up the yappy little dog and put it on her head.

"She thinks Mr. Marc is a toupee!" Brad said, just as the elevator reached the eleventh floor and we all burst out laughing.

Except for Mrs. Leadbetter.

Chapter 3

"This is so cool! It's like a castle!"

Tyler put his disposable camera to his eye and clicked away at the huge building in front of us.

"Uh, Ty," I said, tapping him on the shoulder. "I don't think you're going to get very good pictures standing so close. The museum is kind of big, you know."

Tyler lowered his camera.

"You're right. I guess I could buy a postcard that shows the whole building."

I smiled indulgently. Tourists. Can't live with them, can't put them on a bus and send them home.

It was Tuesday morning, and Brad, Tyler, and I had left the apartment early with Grandpa. We'd walked all the way from Grandpa's apartment to the museum. That's something New Yorkers do that people in L.A. never do. Walk!

Mom and Dad were staying home with Zoey and Mrs. Nelson that morning, helping Mrs. Nelson get used to babysitting an orangutan. Then Mom was going to use the museum's special library, and Dad was going to meet an old friend of his from medical school. We kids told my parents we were going to take a quick tour of the museum, but we were really going to do some investigating. Grandpa had to meet with the museum board on Friday. That didn't give us much time to find out what was really going on.

I grabbed Tyler by the arm and dragged him to one of the museum's side entrances. Grandpa and Brad were waiting for us there.

Together, the four of us went directly to Grandpa's office. Like his apartment, it was crammed with interesting and even bizarre objects from around the world. But it was also neat and orderly. Every book was in its place on the shelves, working files were neatly stacked on the desk, and freshly sharpened pencils stood like tiny spears in the pencil holder.

"Hey, Grandpa," Brad asked, dropping his backpack onto the wildly patterned Turkish rug. "Where's your computer?"

"Professor Hood doesn't need a computer. He has me."

I whirled around at the sound of a new voice. I didn't like what I saw.

Standing in the doorway of Grandpa's office was a very thin, very tall man. His shoulders were slightly stooped, and he clasped his hands together in front of his chest, almost like he was praying. His head seemed shrunken somehow, the skin of his face stretched across the bones. You could really tell this guy had a *skull*—know what I mean? When he caught my eye, his lips formed a smile that looked like a frown at the same time. Was this guy in pain?

The man took a small step—a very small step for a guy with such long legs—inside the office. It seemed as if he thought he wasn't worthy of being in Grandpa's presence. When he moved, I heard a soft, eerie swishing sound. I realized the sound came from the shiny silver material of his suit.

"Kids," Grandpa cried, striding briskly toward the stooped man just inside the door, "meet Mr. Eelio, the museum's assistant director and my right-hand man."

Grandpa grasped Mr. Eelio by the shoulder, and I saw the assistant director stumble under Grandpa's strong grip. The contrast between the two men—Grandpa, with his sparkling eyes and big smile, and Mr. Eelio, with his pained smile and dull little eyes—was amazing. I wondered what Brad and Tyler were thinking.

Before I could find out, Mr. Eelio slid from under Grandpa's hand and gently took his arm.

"Sir," he said, guiding Grandpa toward the desk, "there are some papers you must sign immediately. May I say you look a little tired this morning? Perhaps you should go home early and take a nap or lie down here on the couch and let me attend the staff meeting in your place. . . ."

I shook my head. This guy didn't even stop to breathe! I glanced over at Brad. He caught my eye and grimaced. Good. He didn't trust Mr. Eelio either.

Grandpa allowed himself to be seated at his desk and accepted a huge stack of papers that Mr. Eelio seemed to pull from thin air. All the while, Mr. Eelio continued to talk to Grandpa, but it was as if the rest of us weren't in the room. He kept his voice to a whisper, and all I could make out were hissing sounds. Grandpa also seemed to have forgotten we were in the room.

I turned to Tyler and tried to catch his eye, but he was staring at the wall. No, not at the wall but at a tall, thin girl about Brad's age, standing just to the left of the doorway. How had she come into the room without my noticing?

I cleared my throat loudly. Tyler didn't seem to hear. Brad, too, appeared mesmerized by the girl against the wall. *Okay, what's so great about her?* I asked myself.

And then I saw. The girl stood without moving, as if she were posing. She had long, straight glossy brown hair, parted in the middle. Her eyes were big and brown, and her skin was flawless. When she smiled at Tyler—hmph!—I saw that her teeth were perfect. Hadn't she ever chipped a tooth on peanut brittle, like most of us normal people? Grumpily, I folded my arms. The girl was wearing a small T-shirt and tight hip-hugger pants. Around her neck she wore a choker. It was pink velvet. Gag.

I cleared my throat again. This time, it worked. Tyler's head snapped around. His face looked like a tomato. Brad's mouth slowly shut, but not before a drop of drool had managed to trickle down his chin. He wiped it away with the back of his sleeve.

Something must have caught Grandpa's attention—maybe my extra-loud throat clearing—because he got up from the desk and came to stand between Brad, Tyler, and me and the girl.

"Barbara, I'm so glad you stopped by," Grandpa said in a cheerful voice. "Kids, this is Barbara, Mr. Eelio's daughter. Barbara, meet my grandkids, Brad and Molly, and their friend Tyler. They're visiting me from Los Angeles this week and coming to my retirement party on Saturday night." Grandpa chuckled. "And Molly and Brad have their baby orangutan sister with them, too!"

Barbara sent a sweet smile Grandpa's way and stepped forward. She moved as gracefully as a ballerina. I hated her.

"Pleased to meet you, Brad, Tyler," she said, shaking each boy's hand in turn. Needless to say, Tyler and Brad could mumble nothing more than, "Mmtttt."

Then she turned to me.

"How ya doin', Babs?" I said, grabbing her hand and pumping it vigorously. "Nice choker. Help keep your head on?"

Okay, I'll admit I was hoping to embarrass her. But my plan backfired.

Barbara tossed her shiny hair over her shoulder and laughed sweetly. "You're such a funny child," she said, slipping her hand out of my now-limp grasp.

Grandpa eyed me with The Look. "Yes," he said dryly, "isn't she."

Mr. Eelio, who all this time had stayed by Grandpa's desk, now took a baby step toward us.

"If I may interrupt, sir, these papers await. May I also suggest that my lovely daughter accompany your charming grandchildren and their friend on a brief tour of the museum?"

Barbara walked over to her father and delicately kissed his cheek. "I'd be happy to, Daddy," she said, "but I can't stay past ten o'clock. I have ballet class, you know."

Like *that* was a surprise. I'm not exactly a big person. In fact, I'm kind of thin and short (actually, I prefer vertically challenged), but suddenly, with my wild red hair, clunky sneakers, L.A. Raiders sweatshirt, and jeans, I felt about as sophisticated as an aardvark. I looked at Tyler in his black jeans and black turtleneck and suddenly wondered when he'd become so fashionable.

Barbara looked at Tyler, too, and in her lilting voice said, "Why don't we get started?"

Barbara glided and I clumped through the main hall. The four of us had spent the past hour speeding through room after room of the museum. Brad and Tyler didn't seem to mind not stopping to see the exhibits we raced by. They had eyes only for Barbara, jostling each other to walk directly behind her, jumping ahead to open doors for her, one grinning at the other when Barbara smiled or touched him.

None of them knew or cared if I kept up with them. I didn't even care.

When we reached the front steps, where Tyler had tried to take pictures earlier that morning, Barbara came to a stop. Brad and Tyler bounced off each other and stopped just behind her.

I rolled my eyes, but the gesture was lost. No one was looking at me.

"I have to go to ballet class now," Barbara said. "But I have a wonderful idea. Why don't I take you to the Metropolitan Museum of Art tomorrow morning? Would you boys like that?"

Boys? I thought. *Hello!*

"Thanks, Babs," I said, stepping forward and smiling as insincerely as I could, "but Brad and I have been to the Metropolitan Museum of Art before, and we really don't need you to—"

"Sounds great!" That was Brad.

"Yeah, awesome." That was Tyler.

While I stood there with my face getting redder by the second, and Barbara stood there looking cool, calm, and definitely like the winner, a group of school kids, probably about seven or eight years old, came storming past us.

I couldn't help but be distracted by them. I took one step to the left to get farther out of their way, but that's all I did. I swear.

Next thing I knew, I was flat on my face.

"I'm telling you, she tripped me!"

It was no use. Brad grinned and for about the millionth time chanted, "You're jealous!" Tyler gave me a very mature and disapproving look. What, so now that he dressed like a cool New Yorker he was suddenly Mr. Mature?

After my totally humiliating experience on the

steps—one smart-aleck kid had yelled out to his classmates, "Look, that lady fell *up* the stairs! How stuuuupid!" and his classmates had screamed with laughter—Barbara had gone off to her ballet class. Of course, she'd pretended to be really concerned about me, but I saw what no one else had seen: the nasty little look she'd given me just before she'd turned to go. It was a warning, I was sure of it.

"I think Babs may be involved in the incidents we're investigating," I declared now, as we tossed our lunch trays onto a pile and exited the museum's cafeteria. "And I wouldn't be surprised if her father was involved, too."

Brad snorted. "Barbara? Yeah, right! Her snaky father, maybe."

"Her name isn't Babs, Molly," Tyler said. "It's Barbara. I don't think she appreciated being called Babs."

"Well, I don't care," I responded. "I don't like her and I don't trust her. Besides," I added, scurrying so as not to lose Brad and Tyler as we passed another group of school kids on their way into the cafeteria, "she's too old for you."

Tyler didn't say anything, and in silence, the three of us made our way to the dinosaur hall. We didn't have much of a plan for investigating the strange things going on at the museum, but we figured if we could get the feel of the place today and keep an eye out for anything unusual, we'd have accomplished something.

Anything unusual . . .

"Look!" I grabbed Tyler and Brad and pulled them back to the mouth of a long, darkish corridor.

"What is it?" Brad said, shaking off my hand and adjusting his backpack.

"Look!" I pointed to a guard slumped in a chair. He wasn't moving. His head was bent over his chest, and his right arm hung down. "I think he's been drugged! Maybe he's even dead!"

Suddenly, a huge snort blasted our ears and the guard shifted in his chair.

Tyler shook his head. "He's sleeping, Mol."

"Yeah, try not to let your imagination run away with you," Brad said with a sneer.

I watched Brad and Tyler walk ahead, and then I hurried after them.

"Hey, it was an honest mistake!" I cried.

None of us said anything more until we reached the famous dinosaur exhibit.

"Hey!" I exclaimed. "Do you know why Grandpa's party is going to be in the dinosaur hall?"

Tyler and Brad looked at each other before turning to me. They both had impatient half-smiles on their faces.

"No, Mol," Tyler said, sounding like my mother when she's trying to be patient with me. "Why?"

"Because Grandpa is the museum board's favorite dinosaur!"

Silence.

"Get it?" I nearly shouted. "Grandpa's the oldest guy in the museum, and the dinosaurs are—"

"Yeah, Mol," Brad cut in. "We get it." He rolled his

eyes and turned away. Then he and Tyler both shook their heads and walked into the dinosaur hall. I didn't care if they were too dumb to laugh at my joke—I thought it was funny.

Up until then, my day had been pretty bad, but being around all those dinosaur skeletons made me feel a whole lot better. Not because the dinosaurs are dead—I'm sorry about that—but there's something so cool about seeing the skeletons and imagining what life was like all those billions of years ago. It kind of makes you forget your own troubles. . . .

"Watch out! Move!"

I was standing with my back to the skeleton of a medium-sized dinosaur, reading a pamphlet on the exhibit. I looked up and saw a guard pointing directly at me.

"You, with the red hair," he shouted again. "Move!"

I did move, just in time to avoid being hit by the toppling dinosaur skeleton. I covered my ears with my hands and hunched my shoulders as I crouched about ten feet away from the shower of clattering bones.

I was pretty shaken, so when the bones stopped falling and Tyler helped me stand up, I had to hug him tightly.

"Uuufff," he said. "Mol!"

I stopped squeezing and smiled shakily. "I'm okay," I said. "Really."

"I'll say." Tyler felt his ribs. Guys can be such wimps.

Brad joined us. He'd been talking to the guard, who

had radioed for help to clean up the skeleton and to keep visitors from walking off with a souvenir bone.

Brad looked concerned. "We should go to Grandpa's office," he said. "This is going to upset him, and he might need our support."

We hurried through the museum, our backpacks bouncing heavily on our backs. We reached the hallway where the administrative offices were located. As we approached Grandpa's office, I heard a little hissing noise inside, like someone talking under his breath.

Once again, I grabbed Tyler and Brad, but this time, they must have heard what I'd heard because they nodded. As slowly and quietly as we could, we snuck up to the partially opened door and peered in.

Mr. Eelio was going through Grandpa's desk!

Chapter 4

When we got back to the apartment that evening, I was tired and sore. All I wanted to do was go to bed, but then everybody would have known something was wrong with me. I *never* miss dinner.

Brad, Tyler, and I had not confronted Mr. Eelio. Instead we sneaked back down the hallway, deciding that, for all we knew, the assistant director had every right to be looking for something in the director's desk. We didn't have enough evidence to accuse him of something and run the risk of his getting us in trouble with Grandpa.

Besides, Grandpa had enough trouble already. Now, on top of the other accidents and robberies, he had to deal with the collapse of the dinosaur skeleton. At dinner that night, however, he seemed bothered more by a missing paperweight than by any of the other problems. It was one Grandma had given him on his birthday the year before she died.

"I know it was right on top of my desk," he muttered for about the thousandth time, his dessert untouched.

I saw my mom shoot a worried look at my dad.

"I'm sure it will turn up, Dad," she said. "Why don't

you eat your pie? Mrs. Nelson will be insulted if you don't."

Grandpa picked up his fork.

No one was interested in making Mrs. Nelson any angrier than she was already. Her afternoon alone with Zoey had been a disaster. Zoey had decided it was a lot of fun to swing from the chandelier that once hung over the dining room table. Now, there was a big hole in the ceiling, and as we ate, bits of plaster and dust sprinkled down on our food. From now on, Mrs. Nelson had announced, Zoey would stay with one of us.

The next morning, Brad, Tyler, and I left Zoey with Mom and Dad, and we walked with Grandpa to the museum. When we got there, guess who was waiting for us on the front steps?

Babs.

The next thing I knew, Grandpa was waving good-bye and the four us were in a cab heading east, through Central Park, toward the Metropolitan Museum of Art. I had to sit up front with the smelly cab driver while Barbara sat in the back between Tyler and Brad.

No matter how grumpy you are, being in Central Park on a sunny day makes you feel happy. As we sped along, I watched roller bladers and joggers and people power walking. I saw bike messengers whizzing by and moms and nannies pushing strollers. Young and old, black and white, Asian and Hispanic . . . New York's population is totally mixed. The people can look and behave just as they please. Pretty cool, huh?

The Met, as it's called, is neat, too, but an hour after we arrived there I was back to being grumpy. Although I'd made sure to wear something fashionable today— *my* black jeans, a shiny white blouse, and black cowboy half-boots—I still felt frumpy next to Barbara in her layered slip dress, sandals, and blue velvet choker. Add to that the fact that Tyler hadn't noticed my outfit or really spoken to me once since we met up with Barbara, and you'll get an idea of how my day was going.

I shook my head and hurried after Babs and her groupies. We soon entered the Egyptian wing, probably the most mysterious part of the entire museum. Mummies and gorgeous jewelry and huge stone statues surrounded us.

I had to hand it to Barbara. She did know an awful lot about an awful lot of things. As she launched into a mini-lecture on the Egyptian court and slave system, I tried to pay attention to what she was saying. I ended up imagining what her life might be like. Mom once told me that before you judge someone, you should remember that you have no real idea of what it means to be that person. Maybe if you knew, she said, you wouldn't judge so harshly.

Grandpa had explained at breakfast that morning that Barbara was an only child. Her parents were divorced, and she lived with her father. That was enough to make anyone weird!

Maybe she has no friends, I thought. *Maybe she knows so much about ancient Egyptian culture and Flemish painting because she spends all her time at the museum, by herself.* I was really warming up. *Maybe she's got some horrible disease and knows she's going to die by the time she's eighteen—*

"Molly? Mol!"

It was Brad.

"Man, you are a space cadet," he said, shouldering his backpack. "Come on. We're going to see the Temple of Dendur."

As Brad and Tyler walked ahead, Babs turned to me and laughed.

"Brad's so sweet to take such good care of his baby sister," she said, tucking a glossy strand of hair behind her ear. "But *I'll* take Tyler, any day."

Maybe she's just a snobby cow, I added silently.

By the time we dropped Barbara off at her apartment on West 75th Street, my tongue was numb because I had bitten it so often. I wanted to tell her just what I thought of her, but no way was I going to make a fool of myself again. Unfortunately, there was something about Barbara that made me do and say stupid things.

If only Tyler and Brad—especially Tyler!—could see the truth about her! I'd spent almost the entire day—first at the museum, then at the Hard Rock Cafe for lunch, and finally at Bloomingdale's—being ignored or insulted. How could a fifteen-year-old girl turn a fifteen- and a twelve-year-old boy into such idiots? I mean, they even watched her buy makeup in Bloomingdale's like she was performing brain surgery or something!

I was in no mood to hang around with Brad and Tyler, so when we piled out of the cab, I suggested we go our separate ways inside the museum.

"You know, maybe if we split up we'll have more luck uncovering clues or evidence," I said.

Brad and Tyler seemed eager to check out the planetarium, so we made a plan to meet again at five o'clock in Grandpa's office. *Since when did my supposed best friend become such buds with my brother?* I wondered.

I watched the guys lope off. Suddenly, I felt more lonely than I'd ever felt in my life. Everything seemed to be changing. I had an overwhelming desire to talk to Sloane, but I hadn't brought my computer with me to New York, and I didn't have my mom's calling card in my wallet.

What's the next best thing to e-mail and the phone? A good old-fashioned postcard. I made my way to the museum gift shop and bought a bunch of postcards, some to keep in my travel scrapbook and some to send.

Then I found a seat on a nearby bench and wrote a note to Sloane. It said:

"Hi. Having a good time in NY. It would be better if you were here, too! Don't forget me. Love, Molly."

I smiled and put the postcard in my backpack. I planned to get a stamp from Grandpa and mail the postcard right away. Maybe Sloane would get it before I got back to L.A. I felt less lonely and decided to visit the exhibit of minerals and gems. The picture on Sloane's postcard was of a huge uncut diamond. Now I'd see the beautiful gem for myself.

The mineral and gem hall is dark and quiet. Glass cases display cut and uncut precious stones, all sorts of minerals, and big chunks of metal cut from giant ore deposits deep in the earth. You can learn about the layers of the earth and how they have built up over the millennia—and you can imagine wearing a bright purple amethyst on a chain around your neck. I like the mineral and gem hall. It's peaceful.

That's why I groaned when I saw a school group being led in by a teacher and three class moms. But the kids, who were little, were quiet and well-behaved. I think they were impressed by all the beautiful rocks and minerals and gems. Maybe they were a little scared of the dark, too.

Suddenly, I heard a weird creaking noise. I looked over my shoulder and, for a split second, thought I only imagined the huge, sparkly boulder teetering on the edge of its stand, five feet above the floor.

I never knew my reflexes were so good. Without even thinking about it, I realized that if I didn't grab the little boy, his foot would be crushed. I leaped to the right, scooped him up, and rolled onto the floor—careful to keep him on top of me—as the boulder came tumbling down.

When the crisis was over moments later, I lay on my backpack like a turtle that's been turned on its shell. The boy was giggling on my stomach. He weighed a ton!

The boy's teacher and a hysterical woman who turned out to be his mom picked up the kid and helped me to stand. If I were a greedy person, which I am not, I could have taken a big fat reward from the boy's mother. I remember her saying something like, "Anything you want! Just name it!"

But I wasn't really paying attention to her or to the little boy, who wanted me to "do it again." I was looking past the huge boulder that had toppled from its stand and staring into the dark alcoves at the back of the hall.

I couldn't wait to tell Tyler and Brad what had happened in the hall of minerals and gems—but I had to! Dinner seemed to take forever. Finally, after Zoey, my parents, Grandpa, and Mrs. Nelson had gone to bed, Brad, Tyler, and I met in my room. We needed to go over what we had learned, which, we discovered, wasn't all that much.

Grandpa had told us at dinner that Mr. Eelio, who was still in charge of the so-called investigation, hadn't made any progress. Now that potentially dangerous accidents were happening during visiting hours, Grandpa felt he had no choice but to call the police. Mr. Eelio had promised to file a formal report first thing in the morning.

"Why the delay?" Brad asked.

Tyler shrugged. "I don't know, but I don't like that guy. We need to get some evidence against him, some proof that he's behind the accidents and—"

"But why?" I interrupted. "Don't get me wrong, I don't like Skull Head, either, but what's his motive?"

None of us had an answer to that one.

"Who is going to replace your grandfather when he retires?" Tyler asked suddenly.

Now, it was my turn to shrug.

"I know," Brad said. "Well, I don't really, because no one knows yet. Grandpa told me the board hasn't made a final decision. Mr. Eelio is one of the candidates."

"Would the Eel be trying to make Grandpa look bad so *he* could look good in comparison?" I said slowly, trying to figure out the answer myself as I spoke.

Tyler nodded. "That's possible," he said. "But if he's responsible for the sabotage and the accidents, and if he gets caught, he's in huge trouble. He can forget about being director of anything."

"Except the prison play group," Brad said.

I was getting excited. "But don't you see? People who sabotage museum exhibits and set up accidents that could hurt people aren't normal, no matter why they're committing the crimes. Whoever is behind this scheme to ruin Grandpa's reputation—if that's even his *point*—isn't rational."

For a moment, Brad and Tyler looked at me as if I had just announced I was running for president of France or something.

"What?" I said defensively.

Tyler grinned. "That's the smartest thing I've heard you say in a long time."

I grinned right back at him. "So, tomorrow it's down to business, right?"

"What do we do with Zoey while we're investigating Mr. Eelio?" Tyler asked with a frown.

I'd forgotten. Tomorrow was our turn to babysit!

Chapter 5

"**C**ome on, you guys! Nothing will happen!"

Whenever I say that, someone should immediately lock me in a room with no windows.

Brad leaned on the windowsill and sighed. The sun was bright and the sky was clear—and Brad, Tyler, and I were stuck inside babysitting Zoey. Dad and Mom had forbidden us to take her out of the apartment.

"You heard what your parents said, Molly," Tyler argued. Sprawled in a big, soft chair, he was flipping through a magazine about rollerblading. With his sun-streaked blond hair, his wild-patterned shorts, and his surfing T-shirt, he looked very California. This was *my* Tyler.

"I know, but it's so nice out! Why can't we just take Zoey to Central Park? We'd be with her the whole time. What could happen?"

Brad turned around and gave me a look. Tyler rolled his eyes.

"Aaarrgghh!" I stomped over to another window and leaned my head against the glass. The Hudson River shone in the mid-morning sun. "I can understand why we can't bring Zoey to the museum," I went on. "The last thing Grandpa needs is more trouble. But just to the park—"

Just then, Mrs. Nelson stuck her head in the room.

"I'm going out to the grocery store," she said. "Any special requests?"

I looked over at Zoey, who was sitting on the floor quietly playing with her dolls. I felt bad. I knew she knew she was the cause of my bad mood.

"Yes, Mrs. Nelson," I said. "Zoey really likes those soft oatmeal cookies, the kind with raisins."

Mrs. Nelson frowned, but hadn't she asked?

"Okay," she said. "I'll be back in about an hour."

When the apartment door shut behind her, I tried one more time to persuade Tyler and Brad that we should take Zoey out. I didn't have to try very hard.

"She's gone," Brad said. "I say we go for it. Just one hour in the park."

"You're on," Tyler agreed, tossing his magazine onto the coffee table.

I smiled. "Zoey," I said, scooping up my baby sister, "we're going to the park!"

"Whose brilliant idea was this anyway?" I muttered as we crossed Amsterdam Avenue. The sun was hot, and Zoey was way too full of energy.

"Yours, and don't forget it," Brad answered. "And the next time Zoey insists on being carried, it's Tyler's turn."

"Why me?" Tyler complained. "She's not *my* baby sister."

"I wish Barbara was here," Brad said. "She's cool."

"I wouldn't mind asking her a few questions, myself," Tyler muttered, his head down as if he were studying the sidewalk.

Brad scowled at him. "She's too old for you, Ty."

Tyler's head shot up. He looked totally distracted. "What? Oh, yeah, I know."

Brad looked at Tyler suspiciously before shoving his hands in his pockets and walking on.

We'd left the apartment on Riverside Drive ready for some fun, but Brad and I forgot that Central Park was quite far east of Riverside. To be safe we would have to enter the park south of 107th Street. No New York City cab driver would be likely to give us a ride with Zoey. Ditto bus drivers. And even I wouldn't dream of taking Zoey on the subway!

So we walked over to Broadway, then south to 96th Street. There we turned left, crossed Amsterdam, and were heading toward Columbus Avenue, which was one block away from the park entrance on Central Park West.

"I don't understand why we didn't just go to the park across the street from your Grandpa's apartment building," Tyler said, trying to catch Zoey's left hand. I had her right, but I never felt too secure about a one-hand hold.

"Because Molly didn't want to go to Riverside Park, she wanted to go to Central Park," Brad explained. "Don't you remember that mini-tantrum she threw back on Broadway when I suggested we turn around?"

"Puhhlease! I did not throw a tantrum. Besides," I said, "we're here!"

Before we left the apartment, I'd dressed Zoey in her oldest play clothes so that she could get as dirty as she wanted—or as dirty as she could while still holding my hand. I had no intention of letting her loose for even one minute.

"Hey, it's really beautiful here," Tyler said. "I mean, it's really *green*!"

I smirked as if I'd planted every blade of grass in the park myself. "Didn't I tell you it would be worth a visit? There are ball fields and concert band shells and an outdoor theater and bike paths and—"

"Horses."

I looked to the right, where Brad was pointing at several riders on beautiful mounts.

"Right. Some of the riders from Claremont Stables come here, and the horses that pull the carriages for tourists come through parts of the park down by 59th Street . . ."

If I hadn't been so intent on showing off everything I knew about Central Park, I might have been able to prevent what happened next. As the riders got closer to us, one of their horses must have spotted Zoey—was she waving at him? The horse screamed in fright and reared.

The awful sound startled me. Zoey grabbed my leg with one hand. Her other hand clutched mine tightly. I saw the rider try to keep her horse under control, but it was no use. The horse screamed again.

This time, the sound was so terrifying that I threw my hands over my ears and shut my eyes. I don't know how long I stood like that, but after a while I felt hands trying to pull mine away from my head.

"Molly! Open your eyes!" It was Tyler.

I opened them. Tyler was pale. I saw Brad standing next to him. Brad was green.

About a yard away, the rider of the nervous horse was standing next to him, patting his neck. Her rider friends stood with their horses. All of them were looking at us.

There was only one person missing.

"Where's Zoey?" I asked, my heart sinking even as I asked.

"Mol, she's gone," Tyler said. "Brad and I were watching the horse. I thought it would run at us. We didn't—"

"No," I said, my voice strangely flat and calm. "It's my fault. I let go of her hand when I covered my ears. She must have run away then. She got scared and . . ."

I couldn't finish the sentence. Tears were pouring down my face.

Zoey was gone.

The first thing we did—after panic, of course—was split up to cover as much ground as we could. The riders offered to help in the search. We checked trees and called Zoey's name and asked everyone we saw if they'd seen a one-year-old orangutan running by. Not one person thought our question was strange, but not one person had noticed Zoey.

After about half an hour, we all met back at the spot where we'd last seen Zoey. We thanked the riders and asked them to watch out for our orangutan. They wished us luck and moved on.

"What next?" Brad was no longer green. Now he was brown. He'd slipped in a big pile of mud and horse poop. You don't want to know what he smelled like. For once, I didn't have the heart to tease him.

Tyler's hair was plastered to his forehead. The sun was hot, even under the trees. I knew I had twigs and leaves in my hair. I'd climbed partway up a very tall tree, hoping I might spot Zoey at a distance. No luck.

Tyler sighed. "We are in such major trouble," he said. "How am I going to face your parents?"

Brad snorted. "Let us worry about that."

"Maybe we should try thinking like an orangutan," I suggested.

"I think you already tried that, Mol," Brad said.

"I'm just trying to help," I cried.

"Maybe Molly's got something, Brad." Tyler pushed his wet hair off his forehead. It stuck straight up from the top of his head like a wave.

"What do you mean?"

"Well," Tyler explained, "maybe we should think like *Zoey*. Where would Zoey go if she were on her own in New York City?"

"Now I've heard everything." Brad dropped to the

ground and rested his head on his knees. "She's never been to New York, Ty. How would she know there *was* anyplace to go?" Brad lifted his head. "Except Grandpa's apartment."

Try getting a cab when your brother smells like horse manure. It was hard, but we got one by offering the guy a big tip up front. When we got to Grandpa's block, we had the cab driver drop us off at the corner.

"Over there," I whispered.

Mrs. Nelson was sitting on a bench with a friend. They were eating sandwiches and drinking coffee.

"I'll sneak up to the apartment," I said. "You two keep an eye on Mrs. Nelson. If she tries to come up before I come down, stop her!"

"Right," Tyler said. "Check the hallways and basement, too."

Half an hour later, Mrs. Nelson was still enjoying her lunch and Tyler, Brad, and I were about to run screaming off the George Washington Bridge. I had found no sign of Zoey.

"I think we have to call the police. Or Animal Control," Tyler said glumly as we trooped into Grandpa's building and into the elevator.

"Oh, man, are we history." Brad was attracting flies, and he smacked one off his cheek.

"Don't bring those icky things into the apartment," I said, watching him wipe the dead bug onto his jeans. Ugh.

When we got upstairs, Brad ran to the bathroom, peeled off his disgusting clothes, and jumped into the shower. I did him the huge favor of throwing his smelly jeans and shirt down the trash chute in the hallway. Then I slumped into a chair in the living room and tried to stop myself from crying. Tyler came in from the kitchen, where he'd found a phone book, a pen, and a small pad of paper.

"Look, Mol," he said, "there's no point in moping around. We've got to do something. I'm going to make a list of everyone who might be able to help—"

"What're you doing?" Brad walked in wearing clean shorts and scrubbing his wet hair with a towel.

"Tyler's going to—"

Just then, we heard a key turning, and the front door opened. Mrs. Nelson!

Before any of us could do anything but sit there with our mouths open, Mrs. Nelson was in the doorway. She looked suspicious.

"Well, what are you three musketeers up to?" she asked, her eyes darting from Brad's wet head to the phone book on Tyler's lap.

"Nothing!" I shouted. "Um, I mean, nothing," I said again, this time in a totally innocent, normal tone.

Mrs. Nelson eyed me curiously and then turned to Brad. "Why—"

"I felt really grubby, so I took a shower," Brad said before she could finish her question. "Mom always says, cleanliness is best."

"Yes," Mrs. Nelson replied slowly. "I'm sure she

does." She glanced around the room and frowned slightly. "Where's Zoey?" she asked.

"Taking a nap," Tyler said as if nothing was wrong. He is so calm under pressure! "She didn't really want to go to sleep but we made her. You know how little kids are—first they get overtired, then they get hyper."

Mrs. Nelson raised her left eyebrow and said, "Yes, I am familiar with the crazy behavior of children."

For a minute, I thought we were busted, but then Mrs. Nelson yawned and said, "Well, Zoey has the right idea. A nap sounds good right about now." She turned to leave the room and then looked back. "Stay out of trouble," she said.

"We will," Tyler answered solemnly. "Don't worry about us."

When we heard Mrs. Nelson close the door to her room, I fell onto the carpet and curled myself into a tight ball. "I want to die," I mumbled.

Brad stepped over me. "No, you don't," he said. "Get out of my way." Next thing I knew, he plopped into the chair behind me and turned on the TV.

"How can you watch TV at a time like this!"

"Shhh!" Tyler shook his head at me and continued to scribble down names and numbers from the phone book.

Brad was busy channel surfing. I barely had time to wonder for the millionth time why all guys love the remote control, when an image flashing by on the screen caught my attention.

"Turn back!" I hissed. "Brad, turn back."

He did. Tyler dropped to the floor beside me. The three of us stared at the news reporter standing in front of F.A.O. Schwarz, the largest toy store in New York City. Her mouth was moving, and I knew she was saying a lot of stuff, but the only word I heard was "orangutan."

Then we saw Zoey on the screen. In one hand she held a Curious George stuffed toy. In the other she clutched a Barbie doll dressed as a very pink princess.

"It's her!" I jumped to my feet. "It's Zoey! We found her!"

Fifteen minutes later we were pushing and shoving our way through the crowd of amused shoppers and passersby who had gathered around Zoey on the main floor of F.A.O. Schwarz.

"Zoey!"

There she was, sound asleep, curled up in the lap of a life-sized King Louis doll from the *Jungle Book* movie. She was surrounded by slightly nervous-looking parents, excited children, vigilant store employees, and several TV news crews.

"That's my orangutan!" I cried.

Zoey must have recognized my voice. Her eyelids popped open. She smiled a big orangutany smile and put out her arms.

I rushed over to her and pushed my way into the huge display of stuffed animals. We hugged, and even when I heard one of the cameramen call, "Look at the camera," I didn't. I was too busy crying into Zoey's red hair.

The four of us made it back to the apartment before Mom, Dad, and Grandpa. Mrs. Nelson was still sleeping. As quietly as we could, Tyler, Brad, and I gave Zoey a sponge bath—a real bath would have been way too loud. We dressed her in clean clothes and, one after the other, watched her closely while the others took a shower and changed—Brad for the second time that afternoon.

We hardly said a word until we were all clean and sitting in the living room, pretending to read. Or, in Zoey's case, playing with her princess doll. How could I not have bought one for her?

"What are the chances of Mom and Dad not finding out?" Brad whispered.

Tyler shrugged. "Who knows? I'm not going to be the first to say anything!"

Just then we heard voices in the hall.

"Kids, we're home!" It was Mom, Dad, and Grandpa.

They joined us in the living room. Grandpa looked terrible.

"Grandpa, what happened?" I exclaimed.

Mom helped him to his favorite chair, and Zoey immediately jumped on his lap. Grandpa put his arms around her and sighed.

"Should I tell them?" my dad asked.

Grandpa shook his head. "No, let me. Another guard was attacked last night," he told us, his voice low.

"Thankfully, he wasn't seriously injured, but a very important piece of anthropological evidence was stolen. A very old and precious skull. We were lucky to get it for study. We kept it locked up in a vault. No one has the combination but me. Now the skull is gone."

No one said anything, but I knew we were all thinking the same thing. If the skull wasn't found, Grandpa's career would end in shame.

The phone rang, but no one moved to answer it. A moment later, Mrs. Nelson, fresh from her nap, appeared in the doorway.

"It's for you, Molly," she said.

Tyler, Brad, and I looked at one another. Was it someone from F.A.O. Schwarz? A reporter wanting an interview? I hurried out of the room and picked up the receiver on the phone in the front hallway.

"Hello?"

"Molly? This is Barbara Eelio."

"Uh, hi," I said.

"I just wanted to say how sorry I am your grandfather . . . lost his head." A nasty giggle almost burst my eardrum.

"I . . . you . . ." Where was my big mouth when I needed it?

Barbara wasn't finished. "Your grandfather's been too old for that director's job for years. My father should be the director. As of Saturday, he will be."

"How do you know?" I asked.

I could almost see Barbara shrug. "Because he's the best person for the job," she said. "I've got to go now.

Oh, before I forget, Molly . . . I told Mrs. Nelson to be sure to turn on the evening news. 'Bye!"

The dial tone rang in my ear for about thirty seconds before I remembered to put down the receiver.

I was just turning to walk back to the living room when I heard it. The television.

And then my mother yelled, "Molly!"

Chapter

6

The next morning we discovered that Zoey had made not only the evening news, network and local, but also the front page of every daily newspaper you can imagine—except boring newspapers like the *Wall Street Journal*. Zoey was a star, and I was in the most intense trouble of my life.

But because my parents are cool people, they decided to postpone my punishment until we got back to L.A. Brad's, too. And they told Tyler it was up to him to tell his parents that we took Zoey out of the apartment after we had been absolutely forbidden to do so.

Usually, when I do something stupid and my parents are angry but understanding, I feel terrible, like I don't deserve such nice parents. This morning, however, I felt only determination. We *had* to get to the bottom of the mysteries at the museum!

"What do you think *really* happened to Zoey yesterday?" Tyler said as the three of us sprawled on the colorful rug in Grandpa's office. "Do you think she ran away, or . . ."

I sat up. "Or what, Tyler?"

"Or was she kidnapped?"

Brad shook his head. "Why? And who would do it?"

"People steal animals to sell them to private zoos or research clinics," I said. "Creeps."

Tyler nodded. "Right. But I was thinking . . . what if Zoey's kidnapping and the disappearance of the skull and everything else that's been going on are connected? What if someone knows we're snooping around at the museum, and he—"

"Or *she*," I added. I couldn't help it. I'd told Tyler and Brad about Barbara's phone call the previous night. I'd felt so miserable after being scolded by Mom and Dad—and Mrs. Nelson—I needed some sympathy. Brad had laughed and said I was making it up. Tyler had said nothing.

"Or *she*," Tyler went on, "followed us from the apartment and kidnapped Zoey as a warning."

"Then how'd Zoey wind up at F.A.O. Schwarz?" Brad asked.

"She escaped!" I exclaimed, jumping to my feet. "She tackled her kidnapper to the ground and ran away."

"You are so dramatic," Brad said, standing up quickly. "Maybe the thief just dumped her there. Come on. Let's get out of here before Grandpa gets back from his meeting. Maybe we'll run into Barbara somewhere."

I groaned.

"Okay," Tyler said. "First, let's go say hello to Mr. Eelio. It's an excuse to look around his office."

"I doubt the missing skull is going to be sitting on his desk like a paperweight," I grumbled. The idea of having to spend more time with Barbara made me feel very mean.

"Speaking of paperweights—" Tyler began.

I shook my head. "Nope. Grandpa's missing paperweight hasn't turned up, either."

We headed down the hall toward Mr. Eelio's office. I guess Eel Boy didn't hear us coming. If he had, he wouldn't have been talking so loudly.

"Yes, yes," he said. "The plan is in place."

The three of us stopped in our tracks and stared wide-eyed at one another. Silently, we flattened ourselves against the wall outside Mr. Eelio's office. I held my breath.

"I'll meet you in one hour at Ellis Island," we heard Mr. Eelio say. "I'll be on the eleven o'clock ferry. You'd better have the package for me. Or else."

The receiver banged down. Without saying a word, we raced toward the stairwell. Tyler and I lined up behind Brad, who held the door open a crack, just enough to watch Mr. Eelio leave his office and head for the elevator. We had to follow him. He was meeting his accomplice!

"Come on!" I whispered. "Hurry!"

The three of us ran down the top few stairs of each flight and jumped down the rest to the landing below. Maybe not the safest way to get to the lobby, but definitely the fastest—and the most fun! Our hearts racing, we watched from behind an information desk as Mr. Eelio got off the elevator reserved for the administration staff and headed for the door.

"Quick," Tyler said. "Follow him!"

The bright sun almost blinded me as we raced onto the sidewalk after Mr. Eelio. He hailed a cab and got in. As it pulled away from the curb, we jumped into one that pulled up right behind it.

"Follow that cab!" I cried. I'd always wanted to say that.

The cab driver, who wore a white turban around his head and a long black beard on his face, turned to look at me.

"You are kidding, yes?" he said.

"No, no!" I protested, pushing at his shoulder. "I'm not kidding! Please, follow that cab!"

The driver shrugged, turned around, and put his foot on the gas. "Okay," he said.

I was one hundred percent sure Brad, Tyler, and I were history.

"Cool!" Brad shouted as the cab went up on two wheels to slip between a bus and a line of parked cars.

"Awesome!" Tyler slapped Brad's hand above my head.

"Uh, guys," I said weakly, both feet planted against the back of the front seat and both hands pressed against the ceiling, "do you think this is worth it?"

"Absolutely," Brad said—just before his head made brutal contact with the window to his left. "Whoa!" he groaned, rubbing his skull. "I can't believe I'm in an actual car chase!"

"Dude!" Tyler screamed when we drove through the middle of a parade.

Frantically, I grabbed for a seatbelt. Not there. Of course.

When the driver did a three-hundred-sixty-degree spin on Fifth Avenue at 27th Street, I got down on the floor of the cab and closed my eyes.

It seemed like hours later when we reached Battery Park. Brad and Tyler forcibly pried me off the floor of the cab and hauled me out into daylight. I stumbled. The ground was so . . . *even*.

After the cab driver drove off, I turned to Tyler.

"I can't believe you didn't throw up all over the place," I said. I was feeling a little queasy myself.

Tyler shrugged. "Nope, only on planes."

"There he is!" Brad pointed to a line of people who stood waiting to board the ferry to Ellis Island.

Sure enough, Mr. Eelio was on line, his back to us. I could see the sun shining off his bald head. . . .

"Wait, that's not Mr. Eelio," I said. "That guy is bald. Mr. Eelio has hair."

"You're right," Tyler agreed, standing on his toes and squinting for a better look. "And the Eel was wearing a white shirt. That guy's got a blue shirt on. I guess we'd better get on the eleven o'clock ferry anyway. The Eel did say that's the one he'd be on. . . ."

"I don't get it," Brad murmured, still staring at the man on line. "He looks so much like Mr. Eelio."

Three tickets and three large pretzels later, we were on our way.

"I didn't see him anywhere," I moaned, dropping

onto a bench on the deck of the ferry.

"I checked everywhere, even the men's room," Brad said. "No luck."

"Maybe he keeps moving around and we keep missing him," Tyler suggested.

"Maybe he knows we're following him," I said. "That cab driver wasn't exactly inconspicuous."

"Maybe he's not even *on* the ferry. Did you think of that?" Brad commented.

I stood up again and went over to lean on the rail. How could the day be so pretty—the famous New York skyline looked to me like something out of a fairy tale—and life be such a mess? Grandpa and the museum were in trouble . . . Zoey might have been kidnapped—

"We'll be right back, Mol," Tyler called. "We're going to get some sodas."

I waved over my head but didn't bother to turn around.

I squinted up at the seagulls circling above the boat, and then out to the Statue of Liberty.

And then . . . I was falling overboard.

Chapter

7

"**A**re you sure someone pushed you?" Tyler asked me for the tenth time.

"Absolutely," I said, shivering, even though I wasn't wet. A really cute guy had seen me going over and grabbed my ankles so that only the ends of my hair got soaked. I was shivering because if that guy hadn't been coming around the corner just as I was toppling headfirst into the water, I'd be Molly the Mermaid by now.

"We believe you, Mol," Brad said grimly. "This was for real, even if the guy who rescued you didn't see anyone else by the rail."

The three of us were riding in a cab—a *slow* one—uptown, heading back to Grandpa's office. We had no idea what we were going to do once we got there.

We turned onto Sixth Avenue, and I looked at the crowd of people hurrying along the sidewalk and crossing the streets. New York City is always busy. That's why they call it The City That Never Sleeps.

"Maybe we were stupid to think we could follow Mr. Eelio in the first place," I said with a sigh. "Look at all these people."

"I think we might have been stupid for another reason, guys," Tyler said.

Brad frowned. "What do you mean?"

Tyler looked at us both. "Did it ever occur to us that Mr. Eelio might have set the whole thing up? That maybe the phone call was a fake? That he knew we were listening? That maybe he just wanted to get us on that ferry so he could give us another 'warning'?"

For a minute, no one said anything. The thought that Mr. Eelio the Skull Head might have done something so evil to scare us away from the museum was too frightening. . . .

"I could have been killed!" I finally cried.

Brad put his arm around my shoulder and squeezed. "But you weren't, Mol."

I stared at him with my mouth hanging open, and he took his arm away. Fast.

"So that would mean Mr. Eelio *was* on the boat," I said.

"Not necessarily," Tyler added. "Maybe he does have an accomplice and he's—"

"Or *she's* . . ."

"Or she's the one who pushed you," Tyler said. "Mr. Eelio could have slipped out of the cab at the ferry dock and gone right back to the museum."

Brad knocked on the window with his knuckles. "But we still have no proof of anything," he reminded us.

I frowned, and Tyler sighed and put his head back on the seat.

"What's going on?" I cried.

There were about three hundred people crammed into Grandpa's office.

"Molly?" It was Mom. "Over here."

Brad, Tyler, and I pushed and wiggled our way past the people by the door. Finally, we reached the middle of the room, where Grandpa sat in his big red leather desk chair, wearing one of his best suits. A woman with purple hair was putting powder on Grandpa's face, and a man with three nose rings was spraying oceans of hairspray on Grandpa's wispy gray hair.

"Who are all these people?" I asked.

"Reporters and police, mostly," Dad explained. "There was a ransom note for the skull. It was delivered to Grandpa this afternoon when he got back from lunch."

Before I could even think about the ransom note, I heard a familiar screech.

"Zoey's here?"

"We couldn't leave her with Mrs. Nelson," Dad said. "Not after the chandelier incident. Besides," he added, giving me a look, "Zoey's used to television crews by now."

"Uh, right." Maybe my punishment for losing Zoey wasn't going to happen until we got home, but my parents weren't about to let me forget what I'd done.

I tried to look past my dad, but we both got jostled by a guy with a big news camera.

When I could see again, I burst out laughing.

"What's so funny?" Dad asked.

"Zoey feels the same way I do about Barbara!" I said. "Look!"

Barbara stood by the window, trying to appear as cool as possible while Zoey flipped up the end of her mini-dress. Every time Barbara smoothed it down, Zoey flipped it up again. It's *very* hard to look cool when your underwear is showing.

"Rats," I said as Mom intervened. I could see her apologize to Barbara and take Zoey by the hand.

Then Brad joined Barbara, who gave him a dazzling smile. So that's where he'd gone . . . and there was Tyler, standing a few feet away, staring at Barbara and Brad. Sseesshh! How obsessed was he?

"Grandpa's about to make his statement," Dad said, getting my attention by putting his hand on my shoulder. Mom was standing on Grandpa's left, holding Zoey's hand. Where was Mr. Eelio?

Grandpa stood up and looked bravely at the crowd. I was so proud of him at that moment.

"Ladies and gentlemen of the press, and other friends and supporters of the museum," he began. "It is with great sadness that I confirm the theft of a most precious—"

Before Grandpa could go any further, a horrible scream tore through the room.

It was Zoey.

She was staring at the doorway.

Right at Mr. Eelio.

Mom blushed. She lifted Zoey in her arms and

moved back into the crowd. There were a few chuckles and some excited whispering, and then everybody quieted down again. Mr. Eelio slipped into the room and stood close to Grandpa, his hands clasped in front of his chest and his head bowed.

Well, Grandpa got through his statement and then answered a few questions for the reporters. It was really scary, waiting for a reporter to say something mean to Grandpa, but none of them did. Grandpa is pretty well-known in the city, and everybody seems to like him. What a relief! One guy even asked if he could take a picture of Grandpa with Zoey, the city's newest star! Mom glared at me, but I couldn't help but smile.

Finally, Grandpa excused himself to meet with the board. Mr. Eelio answered a few more questions and then told the reporters the news conference was over. The room emptied out, and the only people left were my family, Tyler, Mr. Eelio, and Barbara. Zoey stood quietly at Mom's side, staring at Mr. Eelio. I wondered if Brad and Tyler noticed how much she seemed to dislike him.

"I'm sorry your trip to New York has been so full of trouble, Mrs. Miles." It was Barbara, sucking up to Mom in a big way. "If there's anything I can do . . ."

Mom beamed. "Why, thank you, Barbara. We need your good thoughts right now."

Barbara nodded wisely. "Oh, certainly."

Gag.

I was losing patience and panicking all at the same time, and time was seriously running out. So far, Brad,

Tyler, and I had proved lousy detectives. If we didn't find some solid evidence soon—

"Zoey!"

"What . . . Get that monkey! She's got my hair!"

It was true. Before anyone could stop her, Zoey had reached up to Mr. Eelio's head and pulled off his . . . toupee!

Chapter

8

"**B**ut, Mom!"

"Molly, I don't want to hear you say another unkind word about that lovely young girl. I don't know why you don't like her."

It was Saturday morning. I was supposed to be helping Mom and Mrs. Nelson make breakfast, but all I seemed to be doing was getting in the way. So far, I'd broken two eggs. On the floor, not in the bowl.

"Okay, but—"

"Molly! Why don't you set the table and let Mrs. Nelson and me finish up in here," Mom suggested.

I sighed, picked up a stack of napkins, and trudged into the dining room. For some reason, Mom was under the impression that Barbara Eelio was a human being. Why wouldn't anyone listen to me when I told them what Babs was really like?

As I set the table with placemats, napkins, silverware, and glasses, I thought again about what had happened in Grandpa's office. I grinned.

After grabbing Mr. Eelio's toupee, Zoey had jumped up on the back of an old leather couch and stuck the fake hair on her own head. It was a scream!

It was also a piece of evidence. Sort of. Tyler, Brad, and I looked at one another. So, Mr. Eelio *was* bald. That guy on line at the ferry . . . Maybe it *was* Mr. Eelio, in disguise. Mr. Skull Head really *was* a skull head!

But we didn't mention our suspicion. Dad got the toupee back from Zoey, and Mr. Eelio slithered off to the men's room to attach it back onto his head. Barbara smiled tightly and, after a nervous look at Zoey, hurried out of the room to find her father.

Still grinning at the memory, I finished setting the table and went to call everyone to breakfast. Mrs. Nelson had insisted we all sit down to eat together at least once a day. Usually, it was fun, but this morning, as I watched everyone gather at the table, I felt glum. Nobody was smiling. Not even Zoey.

We passed around a platter of pancakes and another one of scrambled eggs. When everyone had taken some food, Grandpa cleared his throat.

"What is it, Dad?" Mom asked.

Grandpa smiled weakly. He looked tired, like the strain of yesterday's news conference and board meeting had really gotten to him.

"I was just thinking of the board's decision to pay the ransom if the police don't find the skull before midnight," he explained. "It's one million dollars!"

"That's an awful lot of money, Grandpa," Brad agreed. "But the skull is worth it, right?"

"You can't put a price on a piece of human history," Grandpa admitted. "I just wish the skull hadn't been stolen in the first place."

"At least there haven't been any more accidents," I said brightly. "Or robberies."

Grandpa nodded. "That's true. Nothing has happened since the skull was stolen."

Nothing, I added silently, *except my nearly being thrown overboard into the Hudson River.*

Tyler, Brad, and I hadn't told the rest of the family we suspected Zoey had been kidnapped. We hadn't told them about my close call on the ferry. What was the point? We had no solid evidence. We couldn't prove a thing.

Grandpa sighed and rubbed his neck. "I was thinking," he said, "that maybe I shouldn't go to the party tonight. How can I attend a celebration of what a good job I've done all these years . . . when all I've *really* done is make a mess of things?"

I think we were all shocked to hear Grandpa talk that way about himself. He had to be kidding!

"Dad!"

My mom stood up and threw her arms around her father's shoulders. "Don't even think of not going tonight!"

"Yeah, Professor Hood," Tyler said. "You deserve that party."

Grandpa shook his head. "Mr. Eelio could make a speech for me. . . ."

"I bet that's just what he wants," Brad muttered.

I remembered what Barbara had said to me on the phone the other evening. She'd said that as of Saturday night, her father would be the new museum director.

"Grandpa, you *have* to be there tonight," I cried. "You're the best director the museum's ever had! Please!"

"You can't let us down," Dad added. "We came all the way from California to celebrate with you."

"For my sake, Dad," Mom said, kissing Grandpa's cheek.

"For Zoey's sake!" I added. Zoey put a pancake on her head and looked at Grandpa with her soulful eyes.

Slowly, a smile spread across Grandpa's face.

"What was I thinking?" he said. "Feeling sorry for myself! Of course I'll go to the party!"

We all cheered.

"You are so pathetic!" Brad tossed a foam basketball at my head.

I lobbed it back at him. "Am not! Tyler, am I pathetic? Tyler!"

"Huh?" Tyler turned away from the window. The three of us were hanging out in my room.

I put my hands on my hips. "You've been staring out that window for an hour," I said.

Tyler perched on the windowsill. "I was thinking, okay?"

Brad snorted. "Yeah, I smelled the wood burning."

"At least Tyler has some wood to burn," I retorted. "Hey!"

I dropped to the floor and sat on the Nerf basketball. "You're not getting it back."

"What is wrong with you two?" Tyler shook his head.

"Don't you think we should be figuring out what to do next?"

"Molly only wants to trash Barbara," Brad said, flopping down on my bed. "She's jealous because Barbara's pretty and nice and smart—"

I screamed and put my hands over my ears.

"Well, she *is* very pretty," Tyler admitted. "And smart."

"That's it," I said. "I give up. If you two morons can't see the truth about Barbara, you deserve whatever you get."

"Hey, Ty," Brad said, gazing at the ceiling, "what are you going to wear tonight?"

"I brought the fake Armani suit my mom bought me."

"That's cool. What do you think of a round-collared shirt with . . ."

I got up from the floor—foam basketball springing up behind me—and left the room.

"Zoey, you look wonderful!" I said, adding the final touch to my baby sister's outfit—a purple ribbon tied around Zoey's neck like a choker. It was Zoey's idea, I swear.

Mom had washed Zoey's purple dress three times after my baby sister wore it to her first birthday party and got it covered with cake and ice cream and soda. It looked as good as new. Almost.

"And, Mom, you look beautiful!" I added.

Mom smiled and adjusted her gold-and-diamond

earrings. My mom doesn't get dressed up often—working with primates is a messy job!—but when she does, she's the most gorgeous woman I've ever seen. She wore a long black dress with a big slit up the side, black high-heeled shoes, and the diamond ring Dad bought her on their tenth wedding anniversary. Her red hair was piled up on her head and held in place with a rhinestone barrette.

"You look beautiful, too, Molly," Mom said.

I beamed. Mom doesn't lie. You'll never guess what I was wearing! Mom and I had found it on sale just before we left L.A.—a tuxedo! It was made for a girl, of course, but it was just like a real tuxedo. It was perfect. I could be really dressed up but I didn't have to worry about an orangutan pulling up *my* skirt. Look out, Babs!

I left Zoey with Mom and went to Tyler and Brad's room. I knocked and opened the door.

"Hey!" Brad scooted behind the half-opened door, but not soon enough. I'd seen him in his underwear! "You wait for an answer when you knock!"

"Sor-*ry,*" I said, closing the door a bit. "Where's Tyler?"

Brad yanked the door open. He was wearing pants now.

"I don't know. He said he was going for a walk a couple of hours ago."

"And he's not back yet?" I asked.

"Duh. Do you see him?"

Just then, I heard the front door open and shut. A moment later, Tyler came down the hallway.

"Where *were* you?" I demanded.

Tyler stopped short and stared at me.

"You look great!" he said, surprised.

I rolled my eyes. "Gee, thanks. Sorry it's such a shock."

Tyler shrugged. "Whatever. I was just out." He walked into the bedroom past Brad. "I'm going to take a shower," he said and disappeared into the adjoining bathroom.

"Tyler, wait . . ." I began.

Brad started to shut the door in my face. "Good-bye, Mol," he said with a grin. "See you later!"

The seven of us stood on the street, waiting to hail two cabs to take us to the museum. Grandpa and Dad wore tuxedos, too. Grandpa wore a traditional white shirt and black bow tie, while Dad wore a round-collared shirt with a silver-and-black stud.

Even I have to admit that Brad looked good. He wore a dark suit with a shirt just like Dad's, except that his stud was Day-Glo green. Whatever.

But according to *me*, Tyler looked best of all. He looked fabulous in his fake Armani suit. It was super-dark navy, and with Tyler's blond hair and year-round tanned skin . . .

Hello! I pulled myself together, stepped out onto the street, and whistled for a cab. I had more important things to think about than . . . a boy.

Chapter 9

"**I** have never in my entire life seen anything so outrageous!" I said.

The dinosaur hall had been transformed into a fantasyland. Small, sparkly lights strung above our heads lit the darkened room like stars lighting a night sky. It was eerie and beautiful at the same time.

Tables of food and drinks lined two walls of the room, and waiters and waitresses walked around carrying trays of appetizers. This was my kind of party. Food everywhere!

A string quartet played on a small stage set up just for them. Ordinarily, I'm not into classical music, but somehow it was just right for Grandpa's party.

Get this. When the string quartet took a break, a Peruvian band played for a while. I'd seen and heard a few Peruvian bands on the city street corners, and the music is *so* beautiful. I bought a tape from one of the bands for myself and one for Sloane.

And the people! Some were dressed like my mom and dad, in traditional evening clothes. But some were dressed in ethnic costumes, and others were seriously downtown, hip New York. No matter how they were dressed, everyone seemed to be having a great time.

Tyler grabbed two mini-pizzas from a tray passing in front of us and gave one to me.

"Thanks," I said, after swallowing. "But aren't you lonely for Miss Babs?" I asked sweetly.

About twenty feet away, Brad was falling over himself being Barbara's slave. In one hand, he held a plate of appetizers, in the other, he held her drink. I could see him talking earnestly to her, but Barbara's mind was far, far away. She was scanning the room like she was looking for someone.

Tyler?

Tyler looked at me with the oddest expression on his face.

"You don't get it at all, do you?" he said.

"Get what?"

"Get that I believe you about Barbara."

"Get out!" I stepped back in surprise and bumped into a waiter. "Oops, I'm sorry," I said, grabbing a handful of appetizers still on his tray. I turned back to Tyler and stuffed a mini-quiche into my mouth.

"Well, at first, for a little while, I was kind of, you know, into her," he admitted, blushing slightly.

I snorted. "Tell me about it!"

Tyler sighed. "Anyway, as soon as we suspected Mr. Eelio of being the bad guy, I realized that by staying friends with Barbara, I might be able to learn something we could use against him. I didn't want to use her, or anything—"

"Why didn't you tell me!" I wailed. "All along I

thought you were totally into her and—"

"Uh, no offense, Mol," Tyler said, "but you're not exactly great at keeping secrets."

He had me there. I know about my mouth. Epic.

"So," he went on, "when I visited her apartment this afternoon, I—"

"You what?! You went to her apartment?!"

Tyler nodded. "I told Brad I was going for a walk, but I'd called Barbara to ask if I could come over for a while. I got a chance to look at Mr. Eelio's desk calendar and to go through some files on his desk, real fast."

I put my hands on my hips. "And what did you find, Mr. Sherlock Holmes?"

Tyler reached into his jacket pocket and pulled out a cassette tape.

"This," he said. "I listened to this tape on my Walkman on the way home. There are some very interesting—and very incriminating—ghostly sounds on it. Jake and the other guards weren't lying about what they heard in the museum."

I stared at Tyler and then broke into a grin.

"Wait," he said, grinning back. "There's more."

From another pocket, he pulled out—Grandpa's missing paperweight!

"Mr. Eelio must have stolen it," Tyler said, "and let your grandfather think he'd misplaced it. To make him think he was getting old and forgetful."

"Is it enough evidence?" I asked excitedly.

"I don't know," Tyler admitted, putting the tape and the paperweight back in his pockets.

"Hey, have either of you seen Zoey?"

It was Dad.

"Uh, oh," I said.

"I was holding her hand and suddenly . . ."

Dad looked so unhappy I couldn't even tease him.

"We'll find her, Dr. Miles," Tyler said.

"Would you? And try to hurry. Grandpa's going to make his speech soon, and the last thing he needs is . . ."

Dad wandered off, running his hand through his hair.

"Come on," I said, "let's get Brad. This should be fun!"

But it wasn't. No sooner had we joined Brad and Barbara and told them that Zoey was on the loose than Barbara hurried off, her long, slim paisley skirt floating around her ankles. Brad was left with a long face and two full hands.

"Come on, lover boy," I said. "We've got to find Zoey."

"You totally ruined it," Brad muttered as he dumped the plate and glass with a passing waiter. The three of us began to walk through the room, searching for Zoey on top of dinosaur skeletons and under tables. "Barbara and I were having a really great time."

"Oh, yeah, she looked *so* interested," I said. "Get a life, Brad!"

"You guys, fight later," Tyler said. "Right now, we've got to find Zoey."

He was right. I shut up and followed Tyler out of the

dinosaur hall. We decided to split up and check out the exhibit areas and bathrooms. Guards were on duty to prevent anyone from sneaking into closed parts of the museum, so we asked them if they had seen Zoey.

No luck. After almost half an hour of searching, we met back at the entrance to the dinosaur hall—without Zoey.

"Where could she have gone?" I wondered, biting my lip. "Mom's going to kill us."

"No, she's going to kill *Dad,*" Brad said. "For once, we're off the hook."

We walked back into the party.

"Ssshh, look, Grandpa's going to make his speech!" I whispered.

Up on a small dais, Grandpa adjusted a microphone. Next to him stood Mr. Eelio, a smug expression on his face. Mr. Eelio had stuck like glue to Grandpa all night. Ugh.

Grandpa tapped the microphone, and a screech of feedback blasted through the room. People laughed, and Grandpa pretended to cringe.

After another moment, Grandpa cleared his throat and began to speak.

"I want to thank everyone for coming tonight to share this very special occasion with me," he began. "Especially my family."

"That's us!" I whispered, elbowing Tyler and Brad.

"Oof!"

"Ow!"

Grandpa continued.

"For the past thirty years—"

Suddenly, an inhuman cry—in fact, an *orangutan* cry—filled the room.

"Zoey!" I called out.

Zoey came tearing into the room from the door we'd just entered.

And she was carrying a human skull!

I could see something black stuck on top of it, but it was a human skull, all right. And it looked *old*.

The room erupted in chaos. People shouted and laughed, and through it all, Zoey raced toward Grandpa with Brad, Tyler, and me on her heels. When she was close enough, she leaped into Grandpa's arms. He caught her neatly.

Still clutching the skull, Zoey gave Grandpa the biggest, wettest orangutan kiss any orangutan ever gave anyone!

The crowd roared and cheered.

"Wait!" I cried, pointing to Mr. Eelio. "Look!"

Mr. Eelio stood still as a statue, one hand over his heart.

"How . . . what . . ." he gasped. "How did that creature know where I hid . . ."

Grandpa turned to stare at the Eel. "What did you say?" he said in a shocked whisper.

Suddenly, with a look of panic, Mr. Eelio bolted off the dais.

"Stop him!" I shouted. "Somebody, stop him! He's the thief!"

Chapter 10

"**D**addy!"

Barbara grabbed for her father's arm, but he pulled away and kept running. She looked very scared. I knew in that moment that she had no idea her "perfect" father was a thief.

The crowd around us parted for Mr. Eelio. I think everyone was stunned, but only a few people had heard his confession of guilt. Those who hadn't were probably wondering why the assistant director of the museum was tearing through the room. Those who had heard were probably afraid to grab him in case he carried a weapon.

"Someone has to stop him!" I shouted again. The man was living up to his name. He slithered like an eel through the crowded room.

Brad and Tyler ran after Mr. Eelio. Tyler veered off to the right and headed for a side door—probably to alert a guard. Brad leaped over a chair Mr. Eelio threw behind him.

I wheeled back to look at Grandpa. Mom and Dad had joined him on the dais.

"Is it the skull?" I called to them.

The huge smile on Grandpa's face was answer enough. It was the stolen skull all right.

But where was Mr. Eelio?

I climbed onto the dais and grabbed Grandpa's arm.

He held up the skull, which still wore its black stuff. It looked like a piece of fake moss.

"How could Mr. Eelio do this to me?" he muttered.

Zoey screeched and jumped to the ground.

I felt sorry for my grandfather, but we didn't have time to wonder why Mr. Eelio was so slimy. "Where's the ransom money?" I asked gently. "The million dollars, Grandpa—where is it?"

Grandpa's face turned pale. "Oh, no . . . It's in my office. In the same safe where I used to keep this skull—"

"Then that's where Mr. Eelio's headed!" I cried. "We've got to get there before he does!"

Mom, Dad, Zoey, and Grandpa followed me off the dais. As I ran through the room—by now, the regular lights had been turned on—I heard one of the security guards calling for police backup on his two-way radio.

But what good would the police be if we didn't get to Grandpa's office before Mr. Eelio?

"Quiet!" I whispered as the seven of us sneaked single file down the hall toward Grandpa's office. We had met up with Brad and Tyler in the stairwell. They were out of breath and amazed at how Mr. Eelio had managed to slip away from them.

"That man is truly a snake," Brad said. "Look at this, now I've got sweat stains on my shirt!"

I turned to Brad and put a finger to my lips.

The light was on in Grandpa's office, but that didn't mean Mr. Eelio was inside. For a moment, we looked at one another in confusion. What should we do? Rush the office?

But Babs, in spite of herself, saved the day. She came around the corner opposite us and stopped dead in her tracks. Zoey saw her and immediately broke away from Mom.

Barbara screamed. "Get away!" she yelled.

At that moment, the door to Grandpa's office opened, and Mr. Eelio came running out, his back to us. As soon as he heard his daughter's voice, he turned toward her at the end of the hall.

"Barbara!" he cried.

"Daddy, no! Behind you!"

Before Mr. Eelio could turn around, Brad, Tyler, and Dad tackled him to the floor.

We crowded into Grandpa's office—Mom, Dad, Brad, Tyler, Zoey, and me; Mr. Eelio and Barbara; Grandpa; a member of the board named Mrs. Werner; and two police officers.

"But why?" Grandpa asked. He held up the stolen paperweight and cassette tape that Tyler had found. "Why did you do it?"

Mr. Eelio slid even farther down in his chair and smiled nastily. "Because I should have been director years ago, and I would have been if anyone had had the nerve to make you retire." He laughed. "Then, when you finally announced you *were* retiring, I learned I wasn't automatically going to be made director. The board had decided to interview other candidates for the job that should have been mine."

"But why all the scare tactics? And accidents?" Tyler asked.

Mr. Eelio shrugged. "I wanted to make Professor Hood look bad. So I set up the hauntings and told people it was his idea not to call in the police. The longer the case went unsolved, the better it looked for me."

"But people could have been hurt in the accidents," I said angrily. "A little boy's foot was almost crushed. And I almost got beaned by a dinosaur pelvis."

Mr. Eelio stared blankly at me. He obviously didn't care.

"What about the ransom?" Mom asked.

Mr. Eelio shrugged again. "I took the skull and wrote a ransom note. At midnight tonight, I would have picked up the money at the drop and deposited it in a Swiss bank account. Then I would have pretended to find the skull hidden in Professor Hood's office, where I would have placed it . . . and the rest is easy. I'd become the new director."

Dad shook his head. "Doesn't make a lot of sense to me," he mumbled.

"It made perfect sense," Mr. Eelio said angrily, "until those stupid children and that obnoxious ape got in the way! I tried to scare them off—"

"So *you* kidnapped Zoey in Central Park," Tyler said.

Mr. Eelio smirked. "I'd been following you for

blocks. When those horses spooked, I grabbed the chimp and ran. I knew you'd forget about the goings-on at the museum if you had to find your ape. Everything was fine until she saw the stuffed orangutans in the window at F.A.O. Schwarz. She bolted into the store before I could stop her."

"And what about me?" I demanded. "You tried to throw me overboard on the ferry, didn't you?"

"Molly!" Mom put her hand to her chest. "You didn't tell me—"

"It's okay, Mom," I said. "I never even hit the water. No thanks to Mr. Eelio."

"What I don't understand," Grandpa said, "is how Zoey knew where to find the skull."

"I don't think Zoey knew she was going to find the missing skull, Grandpa," I said. "When she broke away from Dad, she probably just went off on an adventure. She spotted an open door, and when she went inside she found herself in one of the glass-walled exhibits. She was probably just playing around in there when she found the skull."

"And then what?" Grandpa asked.

I smiled. "You do know that Zoey is an artist, don't you? Well, she may have thought the skull looked like someone she knew . . . but without his hair. A piece of fake moss from the exhibit, and voilà! Mr. Eelio. I think Zoey was so proud of her work, she just had to show you right away!"

Zoey smiled, and Grandpa and Mrs. Werner clapped their hands.

"Brava, Zoey," Mrs. Werner said. "Now the museum has its money and the skull, and Professor Hood has his good reputation back."

"Just in time for me to retire!" Grandpa smiled.

Barbara had been leaning against the wall just inside the door. Now she walked out of the room, without a word.

I bit my lip. I still didn't like Barbara—but I did feel sorry for her. After all, it can't be fun learning your father is a criminal! And if the look of shock on Barbara's face when her father admitted to trying to throw me off the ferry was genuine, it meant she finally understood the awful truth about her snaky dad.

I got up to follow her. So did Brad and Tyler.

"Bab . . . I mean, Barbara, wait," I called when I reached the hallway.

Barbara stopped walking. For a moment, she stood perfectly still. Then she turned and slowly walked back to us.

"Uh, I'm really sorry . . ." Brad began.

"Yeah, right." Barbara rolled her eyes.

Brad blushed. "No, I mean it, I . . ."

The look on Barbara's face shut him up. Poor Brad. He really had liked her.

"Are you okay?" Tyler asked.

"I'm just fine," Barbara said, tossing her shiny hair. "Why wouldn't I be? Even though my so-called friend sold my father out."

Tyler looked at his feet. "I was never your friend, Barbara," he said. "And you were never mine."

"Well, we're really sorry," I said quickly.

"Why?" Barbara looked at me as if I'd said the most puzzling thing ever. "You never liked me, and you don't like me now. You just feel sorry for me."

Sshheesshh! Couldn't this girl just say thanks?

Barbara shook her head like she was disgusted with us, then she turned to go.

"Oh," she said, fingering the paisley choker around her neck, "by the way . . . I guess I'll be going to live with my mother." She winked at Tyler. "In Los Angeles. See you around!"

Some people just won't give up. I know. I'm one of them. I stuck my hand in Tyler's and grinned at her departing back.

Chapter 11

"So, Grandpa, have you been holding out on us about a certain person?" I teased the next morning at breakfast.

Grandpa turned bright red! "I . . . uh . . ."

"I knew it!" I said. "You like Mrs. Werner, don't you?"

Grandpa sat up very straight. "Yes, I do," he said. "And she likes me, too."

"Well, that makes it a lot easier, Dad." Mom leaned over and kissed Grandpa's cheek.

For some reason, the idea of Grandpa spending time with a woman other than Grandma didn't bother me as much as it used to. I was happy for him.

"So, what are you going to do now, Grandpa?" Brad asked, shoving a whole powdered-sugar doughnut into his mouth.

"Well, I think Mrs. Werner and I will do some traveling, and then there's the novel I always wanted to write, and then I thought I'd take scuba lessons . . . that is, if Mrs. Nelson will let me."

Mrs. Nelson, who had just come into the dining room with a fresh pot of coffee, playfully smacked Grandpa's arm.

"Oh, yes," Grandpa added, "and I'm going to persuade Jake to take his old job back—with a big raise, of course. I should have listened to him in the first place."

"Who's going to be the new director, Grandpa?" I asked.

Grandpa smiled. "Well, there are several very fine candidates. I'm going to help the board make its decision by the end of next week."

"I want to know what's going to happen to Mr. Eelio," Tyler said.

"Well, first he'll be charged with a variety of crimes, and then there'll be a trial or two," Dad said. "My guess is that he'll spend some time in jail. Maybe even get some help from a psychiatrist."

"Poor Barbara," Mom said, dusting powdered sugar from Zoey's hair. "Her whole life was just turned upside down. First, her father is arrested, and now she has to move to Los Angeles and live with her mother. I suppose that for Barbara the only good thing to come out of all of this is that she'll see some friendly faces when school starts. I hope you kids will be especially nice to her."

Brad, Tyler, and I exchanged a quick look.

"Sure, Mom," I said. But I knew we'd stay as far away from Barbara Eelio as we could.

Dad smiled and said, "You can be nice to her when you stop being grounded, which will be in about ten years."

"But, Dad," I protested, "everything turned out

okay! Zoey even found the missing skull. She's been on TV *three times* in the past week!" I grabbed the morning paper from the floor by my chair. "Look, she made the front page of the *Daily News* again," I cried. "She's famous!"

"And you and Brad can be known as her famous housebound siblings," Mom added. But I think I saw her mouth twitch, like she was trying hard not to smile.

"Speaking of Zoey . . ." Grandpa wiped his mouth with his napkin and pushed back his chair. "I would like to drink a toast to our very own—and very pretty—heroine. To Zoey!"

We all stood and raised our juice glasses or coffee cups.

"To Zoey!" we shouted in unison.

Zoey smiled at us and burped.

Zoey & Me

KEEP YOUR HANDS OFF MY ORANGUTAN!
BY MALLORY TARCHER

Molly's orangutan sister is going away! Now that Zoey is one year old, a faraway zoo has come to claim her. But when the zookeeper arrives to take Zoey, Molly gets the feeling that this nasty woman doesn't really like animals.

Molly and her mom decide to fly with Zoey to her new home. When they arrive, they find out the place is a dump. Worse, Molly overhears the zookeeper plotting to put Zoey into a traveling show to make lots of money. It will take a daring plan to free Zoey—can Molly do it?

ISBN 0-8167-4426-2

Available wherever you buy books.

Zoey
& Me

Don't miss any of Zoey's zany adventures!

THERE'S AN ORANGUTAN IN MY BATHTUB
ISBN 0-8167-4211-1

Molly's little sister, Zoey, is no ordinary kid—she's an orangutan! When Molly's mom brought Zoey home from the zoo, Molly thought having an endangered species for a sister would be great. But that was before Zoey started eating Molly's homework and getting all the attention. Now, Molly's had it with the little orange furball—but what can you do when your sister comes from a zoo?

WHO GAVE MY ORANGUTAN A PAINTBRUSH?
ISBN 0-8167-4278-2

Molly can't believe it. A famous artist bought her painting at her school's art walk fundraiser, and he told Molly she was very talented. Molly is thrilled—until she discovers that the artist has bought a picture that Zoey, her orangutan sister, painted! Should Molly reveal that he spent $500 for a Zoey original? Only one thing is certain: Life stinks when your sister is an ape!

Available wherever you buy books.